JEMIMA
THE PIG
AND THE
127 ACORNS

This book belongs to

I celebrated World Book Day 2022
with this gift from my local bookseller and
HarperCollins *Children's Books*.

WORLD BOOK DAY

World Book Day's mission is to offer every child and young person the opportunity to read and love books by giving you the chance to have a book of your own.

To find out more, and for fun activities including our monthly book club, video stories and book recommendations visit **worldbookday.com**

World Book Day is a charity funded by publishers and booksellers in the UK and Ireland. **World Book Day** is also made possible by generous sponsorship from National Book Tokens and support from authors and illustrators.

JEMIMA
THE PIG
AND THE
127 ACORNS

michael
morpurgo

Illustrated by
GUY PARKER-REES

HarperCollins *Children's Books*

First published in Great Britain by
HarperCollins Children's Books in 2022
HarperCollins *Children's Books* is a division of HarperCollins*Publishers* Ltd
1 London Bridge Street
London SE1 9GF

www.harpercollins.co.uk

HarperCollins*Publishers*
1st Floor, Watermarque Building, Ringsend Road
Dublin 4, Ireland

1

ISBN 978-0-00-852291-9

Michael Morpurgo and Guy Parker-Rees assert the moral right to be identified
as the author and illustrator of the work respectively.
A CIP catalogue record for this title is available from the British Library.
Printed and bound in the UK using 100% renewable electricity at CPI Group (UK) Ltd

MIX
Paper from
responsible sources
FSC™ C007454

This book is produced from independently certified FSC™ paper
to ensure responsible forest management.

For more information visit: www.harpercollins.co.uk/green

For the Merrett family, farmers with the children,
at Wick

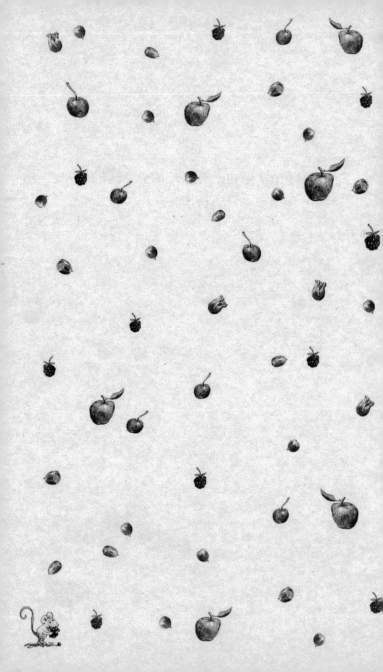

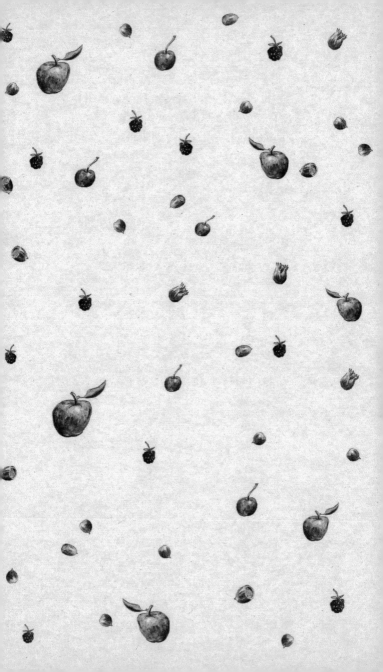

The beginning

I love stories with happy endings. This
one has two happy endings!

Jemima wasn't a puddle-duck –
though there were plenty of those on
the farm – ducks and puddles! No,
Jemima was a pig, a huge black-and-white

Gloucestershire Old Spot sow, the biggest pig on the farm, the biggest pig I've ever seen in my whole life.

And I **loved** that pig.

She smelt, she slobbered, she grunted and snorted and squealed.

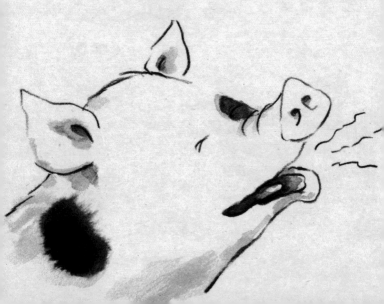

She squabbled with
every other pig on
the farm.

Once she escaped into the vegetable
garden, snuffled up all the potatoes and

chased the ducks

and geese and hens.

She was the queen of Wick Court Farm, and she knew it. She was a pig you don't forget. And my week down at the farm, twenty-five years ago, was a week I don't forget.

I'm thirty-five now, married and with three children, who racket around the place, much like I did when I was young.

In fact, I think that was partly why my mum and dad sent me down to the farm on the school trip, to get me out of the house and give them a bit of peace and quiet. I was a boisterous sort of a boy and I needed room to run and play, and we had only a small garden that we shared with everyone else in our block of flats.

I was ten when I went to Wick. My school was called Burbage Primary School, in London. I still live near there. My kids go to Burbage, as I did. And my eldest daughter, Amy, is going to Wick in a week or two. She's a bit nervous about going away, so I wrote this for her so she'll know what a good time I had down there on the farm all those years ago.

And so this story is for Jemima too. But what's been great about writing this is that I didn't know the ending when I started it. (Actually, I didn't know the ending till Amy came home after her school trip. It was Amy who told me the ending twenty-five years after the beginning happened. I just added it on later.)

The Middle

Dear Amy,

You might think Wick looks like a witchy sort of a house at first, with its five witchy hats, and its fourteen witchy windows, always watching. It's been there

for six hundred years. Queen Elizabeth the
First slept there in one of the bedrooms,
the bedroom where I slept in my bunk bed.
It's called Queenie's Room. (I don't think
she slept in a bunk bed.) The house creaks
a lot at night, almost as if it's talking to you.
It's not ghostly – don't worry. It's just

letting you know it's been there a very long time, just saying hello to you.

You'll see when you get there. But here's what I remember. Around the house is a big garden where you can play on the lawns or climb the trees, and a vegetable garden too, and beyond that is

the farmyard where most of the animals live, the horses and the pigs, the cows and the calves. And beyond that is the moat – which is a bit like a lake that goes all around the house – where the ducks and geese live.

You have to cross the moat over a bridge to get to the farm itself. That's where the milking cows and the sheep graze in the fields, where the apples and pears grow in the orchard.

You're farmers for a week, so you'll

be busy. There'll be no time to miss home.
You'll eat like kings and queens, sleep
like logs and you'll hardly be out of your
wellies, except in bed.

I didn't love everything. When it was cold, we got cold. When we worked, we got tired. And it wasn't easy to be on your own with thirty-five kids and three teachers all around you. And, being an only child, I was used to being on my own. So I'd go off wandering. We weren't allowed beyond the moat, but there were plenty of places inside the moat where I could be alone when I wanted to be.

But after the very first evening I didn't want to be alone. I wanted to be with Jemima. The first time I saw Jemima I didn't see all of her, just her two front trotters, her snout and her great floppy ears. She was looking out at me over the wall of her pigsty. So I went a little closer, not too close, not to start with. I mean, the wall was higher than I was, and she was looking over it. This pig was a giant! For a giant of a pig, she had very small eyes.

She wanted to talk, I thought. So I went up and talked to her, told her who I was, my name, my address, all my details, our phone number too, just to introduce myself. I didn't really know what else to say. Then I told her what a beautiful pig she was. She seemed to like that. We got on really well. But I knew then – because I wasn't stupid, and because she was slobbering – that she didn't want me just to talk, she wanted food. But I didn't know what pigs liked to eat. I asked her, but that didn't help.

Later that first evening, I found out anyway, by good luck. It was after story time round the fire. We were all talking about our first impressions of the farm, of

Wick. And I was going on and on about my meeting Jemima, and how ginormous she was, and how she snorted like this and grunted like that. And everyone laughed at the piggy noises I was making.

Then the teacher, Mr Hicks, said, 'Does anyone know what is every pig's favourite food?' There were lots of silly giggling answers, but no one really knew.

Mr Hicks held up his hand for quiet. 'Acorns,' he said. 'Pigs love acorns. They'll do anything, go anywhere for acorns. They go on acorn hunts, and snuffle up all they can, hundreds. Acorn hoovers, acorn vacuum cleaners, they are. And where there are oak trees, children, you'll find acorns on the ground all around them.

'And this is just the time of year for
acorns, and nuts and berries, of course,
and apples too.

'Autumn. That's when trees and plants reseed themselves. They drop their acorns, their nuts, their seeds.

'We pick what we want, apples and blackberries, and the birds and the squirrels and pigs, if they can, come along and pick up what they want, eat them, drop them, and spread them around.

'Oak trees make acorns, chestnut trees make conkers, apple trees drop apples with seeds inside them. And – Bob's your uncle, abracadabra, lo and behold – a year or two later up comes a little tree, an oak tree, or a chestnut or an apple tree.

'And when an oak tree grows, children, it can grow as high as a house and it can go on growing for hundreds of years. There's one out there just beyond the bridge that's supposed to be seven hundred years old. So it must have been there when Queen Elizabeth the First came here. You remember I told you all about her back at school, how she stayed here in this house, slept in Queenie's room, the dormitory where some of you sleep? I told you all about her, remember? All about Shakespeare and about the Spanish Armada?'

Mr Hicks was like that. He loved to tell stories and his stories often took off in all sorts of weird directions. Here was a story that had started out about acorns being a pig's favourite food, and soon it was about Queen Elizabeth the First and Shakespeare and the Spanish Armada! He was the best of teachers – we all thought so.

Anyway, the next day we went out
on our farm jobs, grooming horses, and
feeding calves, and picking apples. But
best of all I got to feed Jemima, pouring
her sloppy mash out of a bucket into
her trough, and I stood there afterwards,
patting her as she chomped happily away,
snuffling and snorting until it was all gone.
She looked up at me when she'd finished,
mash all over her snout and her ears. It
was as if her little eyes were speaking
to me. 'Thank you. That was lovely. But
where are my acorns? I need acorns!'

And that was why, after that, whenever
I could get away without anyone noticing,
I went on an acorn hunt under the big old

oak tree Mr Hicks had talked about, just beyond the bridge, on the far side of the moat from the house. He was right. There were always acorns there, lots of them, and more every day. On my way back I would stop by Jemima's pigsty and drop over the wall all the acorns I had collected. Soon she was always there waiting for me, expecting me, standing up on her hind legs, trotters on the top of the wall and slobbering in happy anticipation. She'd let me scratch her cheek, pat her neck.

Day after day I fed her. There was one day when I collected so many acorns that all my pockets were stuffed with

them, bulging with them. A hundred and twenty-seven, I counted, my most ever!

So Jemima had a feast of acorns that day. But she had soon snuffled them all off the ground, and then stood up, trotters on the wall, asking for more, or saying thank you, or both.

'Tomorrow,' I told her.

But when tomorrow came there was terrible news. Jemima was sick, the farmer told us when we came out to work after breakfast. She was lying down and couldn't seem to get up. The farmer couldn't understand it. It looked as if she'd eaten something poisonous, he said, like too many acorns. Acorns were fine, the farmer told us, their favourite food, but if

she'd eaten too many, then they could be dangerous. But he didn't think it could be acorns, because she hadn't escaped recently, so far as he knew. So how could she have got acorns? The vet had been called. I didn't dare look up. We all went very quiet. I wasn't the only one who loved Jemima. But I was the only one who had fed her pocketfuls of acorns.

We were all told we had to stay away from the pigsty, that they'd let us know how she was when the vet had been. I was out in the garden when the vet came. I watched her going into the pigsty with the farmer. I had to get closer, I had to find out. I found a place in the vegetable garden where I could crouch down and not be seen. I was full of tears inside. I

could hear Jemima moaning and groaning.
I knew she must be in such pain, and I
knew I had been the cause of it.

Then I saw the vet standing up, and
then the farmer. They were both laughing.
And each of them was holding up a tiny
little squealing piglet.

'How many is that?' said the farmer.

'Fifteen,' the vet told him. 'No wonder Jemima was feeling so bad.'

'I didn't even know she was having them,' the farmer said. 'She's like that, Jemima is. She likes to keep things to herself.'

Later that day we were all allowed to go and have a look. There we were, peering over the wall into the pigsty, and there she was feeding her piglets, fifteen of them, squirming, squeaking, clambering over each other to feed, and I could see she was loving it all, loving them all, as much as I knew she loved acorns. But that was our secret.

I had this great idea before I left. I

wanted to take some acorns home, to plant one in our garden at home, and maybe lots down the road in the park. That way I could take a little bit of Wick with me. So, early in the morning on the day we left, I crept out in my pyjamas, ran out across the yard and over the bridge to the old oak tree, where I stuffed my dressing-gown pockets full of acorns.

On the way back I went to see Jemima to say goodbye. She was waiting for me. I gave her one acorn out of my hand, told her that was enough, told her she was a very clever mother, and that I loved her, and would never forget her. I was teary then when I left her.

As we were getting on the bus, Mr Hicks saw I was still teary. He smiled at me. Then he said: 'Acorns. Your pockets, they're stuffed, aren't they? Did you leave any? I was out this morning myself, early, saw you picking them up. They belong here really,' he went on. 'Best to let them stay here, grow here. What do you think? Take one home if you like, just one, that'll be fine.' I knew he was right.

I went over to the corner of the field by the bridge and scattered them out on to the grass, emptied my coat pockets. I kept one for the garden at home, planted it as soon as I got back. It never grew. I expect a squirrel had it.

So that was the first ending of my story, the story I wrote and gave to Amy, to read on the bus on her way to her school trip to Wick all these years later.

Now here's the second ending, which is much better, the ending she told me when she got home.

The ending

When Amy got off the coach, she didn't even say hello or give me a hug. She was breathless to tell me. The words were tumbling out of her as we walked home.

'Dad, you're not going to believe this. But you know in that story you gave me, all about Jemima and those a hundred and twenty-seven acorns, about how that teacher, Mr Hicks, made you leave behind those acorns you stuffed into your coat pocket before you left Wick, and how he told you you should really leave them where they belonged and throw them all out in the corner of the field, by the bridge?

'Well, they grew. They're trees now, Dad, proper trees, ten of them, like a little forest, some of them twice as tall as you. So you planted a forest, Dad. And, and, and do you know, Dad, Dad, they still have Gloucestershire Old Spot pigs on the farm? The farmer told me they're still from the same family as Jemima. He remembers Jemima, and the fifteen piglets. It was a record. No pig has ever had so many piglets since in one go. I told him all about the hundred and twenty-seven acorns, and he laughed so much he shook all over.'

I hardly knew what to say. It was so good to have her home, and to have her ending. Far better than mine. So I added it on to my story. She didn't seem to mind. And she agreed that it does make it a far better story.

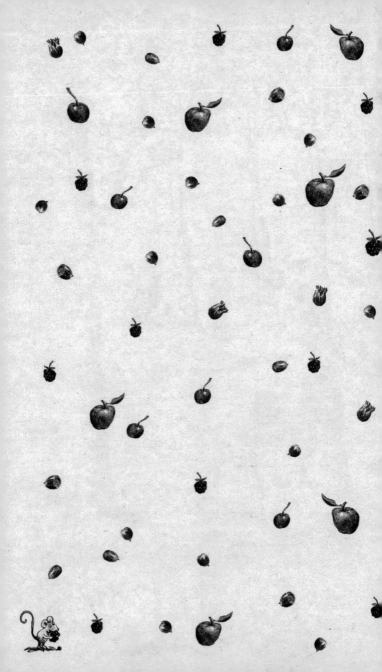

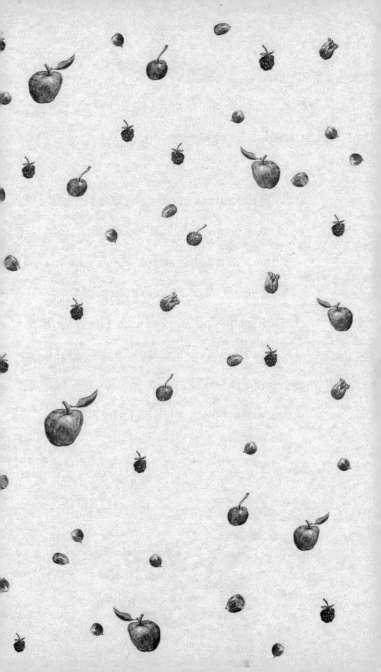

From the author of the story you've just read, master storyteller Michael Morpurgo, and illustrated by the award-winning Emma Chichester Clark, comes a surprising, charming and uplifting twist on *The Wizard of Oz*, told by a very special and unforgettable character: Dorothy's pet dog, Toto. Read on for an extract from this wonderful book . . .

michael morpurgo

TOTO

THE WIZARD OF OZ

as told by the dog

illustrated by Emma Chichester Clark

PROLOGUE

———◆———

I Was There...

*T*hat was how Papa Toto always began his story: "I was there." There were seven of us puppies, and that's a lot, and I was the littlest. Papa Toto always called me Tiny Toto. Whenever Mama lay down in the basket to feed us, my brothers and sisters just trampled all over me to get to her first. Mama hardly noticed me, I was so small, but Papa Toto did. He always saw to it there was a proper place for me, and when the others pushed me off, he'd nose them away to make room for me. Without Papa Toto

I guess I wouldn't ever have had enough milk, would probably never have lived to grow up at all and tell the tale.

Papa Toto's tale was the best part of every day for me. Papa Toto would wait till Mama had climbed out of the basket and gone out of the house with all the people folk. Like Dorothy, who Papa Toto loved almost as much as he loved me. And that wasn't just because I was the littlest and the best-looking but because I was the only one who was always still awake at the end of his story. We didn't see too much of him during the day. He was out most of the day on the farm working alongside Dorothy and Uncle Henry and Aunt Em, ploughing and sowing. Of course, Papa Toto didn't do all the chores himself – that was people folk's work – but he did drive the cows, keep an eye out for snakes and wolves and the like, and chase rabbits and rats and mice whenever and wherever he found them.

And on the lazy hot days he'd just hang around, making sure Dorothy didn't come to harm. "It's what I'm for," he'd tell us. "Wherever she goes, I go. But now you littl'uns are around, Dorothy says I got to look after you from time to time, give your mama a break from you. But I don't want none of your wriggling and clambering and tumbling out like you do, and no chewing on my tail. No piddling in the basket, y'hear. Dorothy don't like it when you piddle on the floor neither. And don't go pestering me for food, cos you ain't going to get none – I've told you time and again that's what your mama does, not me. You just lie still and go to sleep."

But lying still only ever happened when we were all fast asleep, and Papa Toto had his own special way of getting us to do that. He'd be telling us one of his stories, and, sure enough, pretty soon all the wriggling and clambering and the tumbling stopped, and we'd all be lying there still and listening, all seven of us. And then, one by one they'd all drop off to sleep and in the end I'd often be the only one left awake, because I always wanted to hear what happened in the end. The way I saw it, there wasn't much point in listening to the beginning of the story if you didn't hear how it finished. Of course, I knew *what happened in the end – we had all heard Papa Toto's stories often enough. But it was the way he told them that kept me awake, kept me listening, like he was there inside the story and I was right there with him.*

Even so, I've got to say – but don't you go telling him now – I did drop off during some of his tales. But there was one story I stayed awake to hear from beginning to end, the one about the Wizard of Oz, the one he always began with: "I was there." Papa Toto especially loved telling that story, and we loved hearing it. The way he told it you just had to believe every last word of it. Of course, I never believed it afterwards. But I wanted to. It was funny and frightening, and sad and silly, and weird and wonderful, and so amazing and exciting that I never wanted to go to sleep, however warm and snug and full up with milk I was. That was Papa Toto's best tale, the one I longed for, the one I never fell asleep in. He'd climb into our basket in the corner of the room, turn round and round, and then lie down carefully, trying not to squash any of us, but he always did, and this time it was me.

"Sorry, Tiny Toto," he said, nudging me gently with his cold, cold nose. He waited until all the squealing and squeaking had stopped, till we were all snuggled up to him, and ready for the story.

"I was there," he began, and those magic words sent shivers down my spine. It was going to be the wizard story. "Dorothy and me were both there. She never tells Uncle Henry or Aunt Em this story any more, because they won't believe her. She told me that one day, when she has children of her own, she'll tell them, because children know how to believe. Well, pups are children too, right? So I can tell you. Think of that: you little pups will know this story before any people folks know it, except Dorothy, of course, and me."

We were all silent, snuggled up together, all of us lying there, waiting, waiting. Then Papa Toto began.

"Well, little pups, my tale begins in this very house, in this very room, in this very basket…

CHAPTER ONE

———◆———

A Giant Monster
of a Twister

I *was lying right here, deep in my dreams in* *this very basket, when I was woken up by the* sound of the wind roaring and howling around the house, rattling the doors and windows, shaking the whole place. I never heard a wind like it. The door blew open. So I got up and went outside. Everyone was rushing round, Dorothy trying to shut the hens into the hen house, but they were skittering about all over the place.

They didn't want to go inside, of course they didn't. It wasn't getting dark yet. The hens never go to bed before dark. What was Dorothy thinking of? Uncle Henry was driving the cattle into the barn, but they didn't want to go in either, and he was calling for me to come and help him, but I had sleep still in my head and didn't want to. Anyway, he was managing well enough on his own, I thought, without me. Aunt Em was trying to shut the barn doors, but the wind wouldn't let her. She was blown off her feet and went rolling over and over, like tumbleweed. Dorothy saw what was happening, left her hens and ran to help Aunt Em up on to her feet, and together with Uncle Henry they managed to shut the barn door.

Then they did some more chasing round, getting old Barney, our plough horse, into his stable, rounding up the pigs – and that wasn't easy either – and all the while they were hollering at each other about a great storm coming in, and how the clouds were dark in the north and how that was a bad sign.

If I'm not mistaken, there's a twister on the way," Uncle Henry was bellowing. "I'll eat my hat else."

And then suddenly he didn't
have any hat on his head any more.
It had blown away. So I went after it.

I love a good old hat chase, especially when there's a wind blowing over the prairies in Kansas. As Uncle Henry often says, maybe other folks in other places invented the wheel and writing and all that clever stuff, but in Kansas we invented the wind.

Anyways, I went chasing that hat of Uncle Henry's just about all over Kansas, and caught up with it down by the creek where it landed in the water, and I dived right in, grabbed it in my teeth and trotted back home, head high, tail high, pretty darned pleased with myself.

I've always been like that. If I'm chasing after something, hats especially, I put just about everyone and everything else out of my mind. But now the chase was over and I could hear Dorothy screaming for me to come home. I could see her now, standing on the veranda of the farmhouse, and right behind her and nearly right above her came this giant monster of a twister just a-roaring and a-raging, towering up into the sky, taking the barn with it, making splinters of it, and the fences too, and the rain tub, swirling and swallowing the lot. Well, I ran. I took the steps up the veranda in one bound, jumped right into Dorothy's arms.

"Where've you been, Toto?" she cried, hugging me to her and running into the house.

I showed her the hat in my mouth, shook it for her to be quite sure she noticed how clever I had been!

"You rescued Uncle Henry's hat!" I was so pleased that she was pleased. "You are such a clever Toto. Don't you drop it now. We got to get ourselves safe out of this storm, else we'll be blowed to smithereens. Aunt Em and Uncle Henry are waiting for us down in the cellar. But I couldn't really leave you behind, could I? I ain't going down there without Toto, I told them. And now I got you, that's where we're going, right now. I know you don't like it down in the dark, Toto, but it's safe down there, so like it or lump it, you're coming with me."

She was right, I hated it down in that cellar. Never did like the dark, still don't. I could see the trapdoor open on the far side of the room. I could hear Aunt Em and Uncle Henry hollering for us to hurry up. Dorothy managed to get the front door shut against the wind, with the house shaking all around us, shaking so bad I thought that old twister was going to make splinters of it any moment. Cups and saucers, jugs and plates, smashed on to the floor. Drawers flew open, knives and forks and spoons, kettles and pots and pans, rattled and crashed, chairs and cupboards and dressers tipped over.

I was never so scared in all my life. We were halfway across the room when the strangest thing happened. The trapdoor slammed itself shut, and all of a sudden the shaking and the roaring, the whistling and wailing, simply stopped. I heard Aunt Em and Uncle Henry still calling for us from down below in the cellar, but their voices were becoming fainter with every moment.

Then all was silence.

The whole house was
swaying now, and we were
swaying with it. Dorothy fell on
to her knees but never let go of me.
She crawled to her bed in the corner,
and we curled up there, holding on
to one another, wondering what had
happened, what was going to happen.

"We're floating, Toto!" Dorothy cried.
"Floating on the air right in the middle
of the twister. We're flying, Toto."
She called out for Aunt Em
and Uncle Henry. But
there was no reply.

"We're all alone," Dorothy said, her voice trembling a bit. "But don't you worry none. I'll look after you, Toto. You know I will."

And I did know that, so I wasn't worried, not as much as I had been anyway. There was blue sky outside the window now, and we were flying up and out of the clouds. There was hardly a sound. I wasn't frightened at all any more. I did feel a little sick though, what with all this floating about in the air, especially when the house lurched and tipped and rocked about.

"We'd best lie down, Toto," said Dorothy, "and close our eyes, then we'll feel better."

So that's what we did, and pretty soon, what with all that gentle swaying and rocking, we were both of us fast asleep, her arm around me, my head in her lap, Uncle Henry's hat right beside me. She'd told me to look after his hat, so that's just what I was doing . . .

Happy
World Book Day!

As a charity, our mission is to encourage every child and young person to enjoy reading, and to have a book of their own.

> Everyone is a reader — that includes you!

Whether you enjoy **comics**, **fact books**, **adventure stories**, **recipes** – books are for everyone and every book counts.

On **World Book Day**, everyone comes together to have **FUN** reading. Talking about and sharing books with your friends and family makes reading even more memorable and magic.

Illustration by Allen Fatimaharan © 2021

Where will your **reading journey** take you next?

1 **Take a trip to your local bookshop**
Brimming with brilliant books and helpful booksellers to share awesome reading recommendations, bookshops are magical places. You can even enjoy booky events and meet your favourite authors and illustrators!

Find your nearest bookseller at booksaremybag.com/Home

2 **Join your local library**
A world awaits you in your local library – that place where all the books you could ever want to read await. Even better, you can borrow them for **FREE**! Libraries can offer expert advice on what to read next, as well as free family reading events.

Find your local library at gov.uk/local-library-services

Scan here to visit our website!

3 **Check out the World Book Day website**
Looking for reading tips, advice and inspiration? There is so much to discover at worldbookday.com/getreading, packed with book recommendations, fun activities, audiobooks, and videos to enjoy on your own or as a family, as well as competitions and all the latest book news galore.

Books by Michael Morpurgo